HOW TURTLE'S BACK WAS CRACKED

A TRADITIONAL CHEROKEE TALE

RETOLD BY
GAYLE ROSS

PAINTINGS BY
MURV JACOB

DIAL BOOKS FOR YOUNG READERS NEW YORK

For my children, Alan and Sarah—G.R.

For Jana, Holly, Roxanne,
and Nick—I love you kids!—M.J.

Published by Dial Books for Young Readers
A Division of Penguin Books USA Inc.
375 Hudson Street
New York, New York 10014

Designed by Julie Rauer
Printed in Hong Kong
First Edition
1 3 5 7 9 10 8 6 4 2

Library of Congress Cataloging in Publication Data
Ross, Gayle.
How Turtle's back was cracked : a traditional Cherokee tale /
retold by Gayle Ross; illustrated by Murv Jacob.—1st ed.
p. cm.
Summary: Turtle's shell is cracked when the
wolves plot to stop his boastful ways.
ISBN 0-8037-1728-8 (trade).—ISBN 0-8037-1729-6 (library)
1. Cherokee Indians—Legends. 2. Tales—Southern States.
[1. Cherokee Indians—Legends.
2. Indians of North America—Legends. 3. Turtles—Folklore.]
I. Jacob, Murv, ill. II. Title. E99.C5R67 1995 398.2—dc20
[E 089975075] 93-40657 CIP AC

The artwork was rendered in acrylics
on watercolor paper.

AUTHOR'S NOTE

I have known this story since I was small. When I decided
to retell it as a storyteller, I looked for written sources and
found the legend, in a very skeletal form, in James Mooney's
Myths of the Cherokee, published in 1900 by the Bureau of
American Ethnology. My version of the tale grew out of years of
actually telling the story to audiences of all ages. I have made no
essential changes to the story as it appears in Mooney; I have
merely added detail and character development consistent
with the culture from which the story springs.

This is what the old people told me when I was a child, about the days when the people and the animals still spoke the same language. Now, in those days Possum and Turtle were best friends. Many people thought it odd that two such very different creatures would be so close, but Possum and Turtle knew they had a lot in common. Neither of them liked to go anywhere in a hurry, and they both loved persimmons.

Here is how they shared persimmons together. Possum
would climb a persimmon tree, wrap his strong tail around a
limb, and hang. Turtle would come and stand at the foot of the
tree, and Possum would swing up and pick a persimmon for
himself and eat it. Then he would swing up and pick another
one, and Turtle would open his mouth as wide as it would go.
Possum would take careful aim and drop the persimmon into
Turtle's mouth. They could do this for hours.

They were sharing persimmons in this way one day, when a wolf came along. The wolf watched the two friends for a while, and he saw a way to play what he thought was a pretty funny joke and get a free lunch all at the same time.

He went and he stood behind Turtle, and when Possum dropped a persimmon, the wolf leaped into the air and snatched it before it could land in Turtle's mouth. When Turtle opened his mouth, he closed his eyes, so he did not see the wolf; all he knew was that he saw Possum drop the persimmon, but it didn't land in his mouth. And after he saw many, many persimmons dropped that he did not eat, Turtle began to get angry.

"Possum, up in the tree, saw the wolf and realized what was happening. Now, if you have a best friend, and you're trying to make a present to him, and someone comes along and steals it, it can make you angry. And that's how it was with Possum. He decided to fix that wolf. He looked all around the tree and found the biggest, ripest persimmon he could find.

Then, instead of just dropping the persimmon down to Turtle, he threw it with all the strength he had, and the greedy wolf leaped into the air with his mouth wide open. The persimmon flew down his throat and stuck there, and he choked to death. Possum thought no more about it. He went back to eating persimmons.

When Turtle opened his eyes and saw the dead wolf, he realized where his persimmons had gone. And the more he thought about how the wolf had stolen his food, the angrier he became. He began to scold the wolf, saying, "You were a very greedy wolf! You got what you deserved!" Then he said, "Possum and I sure showed you! You won't be stealing any more persimmons." And then, "That was a very brave thing for me to do!" And finally he convinced himself that he alone, Turtle the Mighty Hunter, had slain the greedy wolf.

Now, it is a custom for a hunter to take what is called a tribute from an animal he has killed. In this way he captures a piece of the animal's spirit, which then belongs to him. Turtle decided he had the right to take a tribute from the dead wolf, so he cut off the wolf's ears. He took them home and fixed them onto two long wooden sticks and made wolf-ear spoons.

In the old days it was another custom to offer a visitor food to eat the very first thing. And there was a special dish that was usually kept cooking at all times just to offer a guest. This was a kind of thick corn soup. Turtle took his wolf-ear spoons and went visiting.

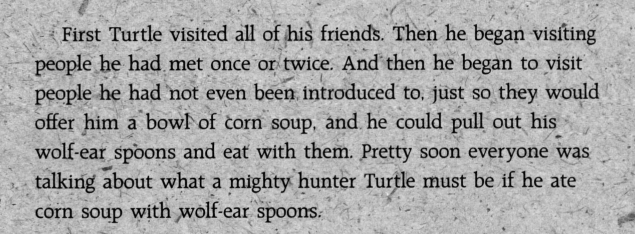

First Turtle visited all of his friends. Then he began visiting people he had met once or twice. And then he began to visit people he had not even been introduced to, just so they would offer him a bowl of corn soup, and he could pull out his wolf-ear spoons and eat with them. Pretty soon everyone was talking about what a mighty hunter Turtle must be if he ate corn soup with wolf-ear spoons.

It wasn't long before word got back to the rest of the
wolves, and they were angry. This was a terrible insult, for
such an insignificant creature as Turtle to be eating corn soup
with wolf-ear spoons. The wolves decided Turtle must die.
Now, wolves are faster than turtles, and they had no

trouble catching Turtle. But then, in the manner of wolves everywhere, they began to argue over what to do with him. Turtle listened, and decided that the only thing he could do would be to keep his wits about him, and be ready for any chance that he saw.

Finally one wolf said, "I know what we'll do with you, Turtle. We'll build a roaring fire, throw you in it, and burn you alive." Turtle thought very quickly and said, "Oh, please do. I'd love it. You see these big strong feet? I could stamp out every spark of your fire before I even got warm."

Well, the wolves didn't like that, and so they argued some more. Finally one of the wolves said, "I have an idea. Turtle, we'll build that roaring fire. We'll put a clay pot of water on the fire, throw you in, boil you, and make turtle soup!"

Turtle thought very quickly and said, "Oh, please do. I'd love it. You see these big strong feet? I could stamp your pot to pieces before the water could get warm!"

The wolves didn't like that either. They argued and argued, and finally one wolf said, "Well then, Turtle, I know what we'll do with you. We'll carry you down to the deepest part of the river and throw you in. We'll stand on the bank and watch you drown!" And Turtle thought very quickly and said, "Oh, no, not the river! Anything but the river!"

Well, as soon as the wolves heard that, of course they carried Turtle down to the riverbank.

They threw him into the water as hard as they could, which should have been fine. Turtles live in the river. But Turtle didn't land in the water the way he thought he would. The wolves threw him so hard, he went spinning end over end as he fell, and he landed on his back on a rock in the middle of the river, and then he bounced into the water.

As Turtle swam to the other side of the river, he could feel his back shifting and moving. When he crawled out of the water and looked over his shoulder, he saw that his beautiful shiny shell had been cracked into a dozen pieces.

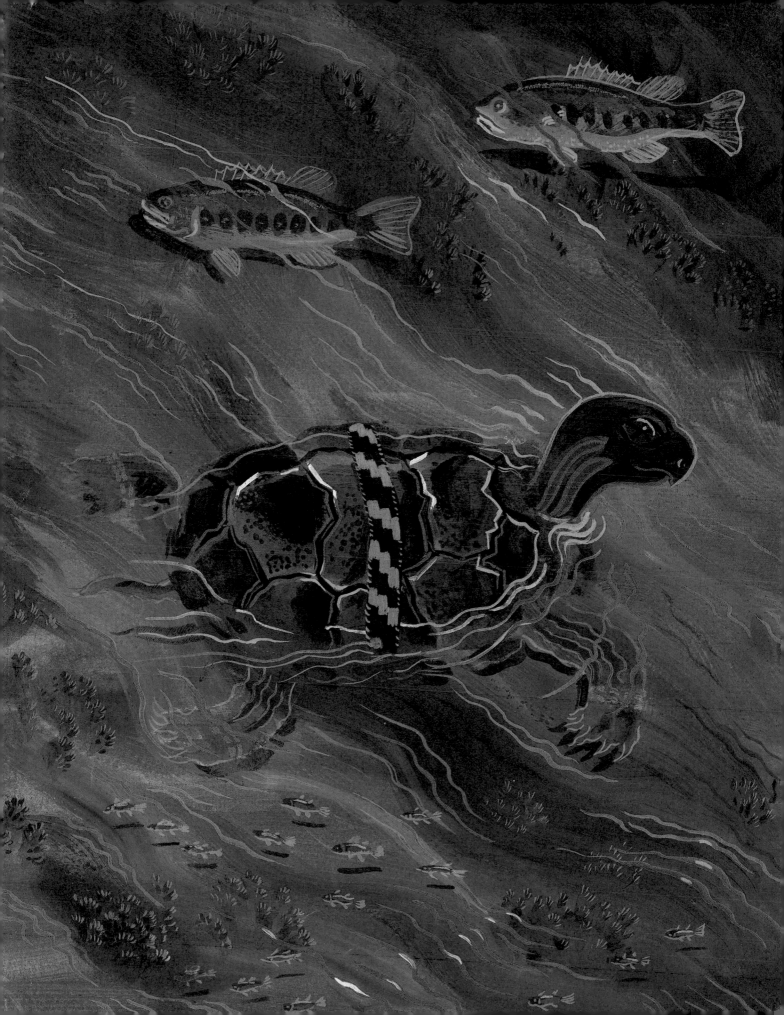

Now, Turtle wasn't a mighty hunter, but he was a very good doctor. He knew many conjuring secrets. He knew the healing plants and how to prepare them. When he had gathered all the plants he needed, he went about the business of doctoring himself, singing, *"Gû'daye'wû, Gû'daye'wû* (GUNH-dah-YAY-wunh). I have sewn myself together, I have sewn myself together."

And over the time that has passed from that day to this, Turtle's shell has grown strong again. But if you look closely, you can still see the lines where Turtle's back was cracked, and you will never see another turtle eating corn soup from wolf-ear spoons.

THE CHEROKEE NATION

For over four hundred years we have been known as the Cherokee, though the word is of foreign origin. In our own language we are Ani Yun Wiya (Ah-NEE Yuh Wee-YAH), The Real People. Once the largest and most powerful of the Southeastern tribes, the Cherokee lived in harmony with their world in the mountains now called the Smokies. Their powerful matrilineal clan system was balanced by a strong hunter-warrior tradition.

In the 1800's they were perhaps the most famous of all the American Indian nations, known for their efforts to live in peace with their white neighbors. The Cherokee had adopted a written constitution. The Cherokee genius Sequoya had developed a syllabary, making it possible for the people to read and write in the native language. A newspaper printed in English and Cherokee was begun. But these great accomplishments did not protect the Cherokee from the holocaust known as Indian Removal, Andrew Jackson's policy of forcing the Southeastern tribes from their homes to lands west of the Mississippi. Over four thousand Cherokee people lost their lives on the forced march to the west in the winter of 1838-39. The long walk came to be known as the Trail of Tears.

Today the Cherokee people make up the second largest Indian nation in the United States, with a national capital in Tahlequah, Oklahoma. The Cherokee language is spoken and taught widely, and the traditional dances, such as the stomp dances, are still held.   —G.R.